Presented to the LosAltos Library

from   Vera Albuquerque

PALO ALTO
   CALIFORNIA

24th Feb 1994 .

THE HIDDEN GIFT

THE HIDDEN GIFT

by

Vera Albuquerque

A Bookland Juvenile

Carlton Press, Inc.   **New York, N.Y.**

THE HIDDEN GIFT

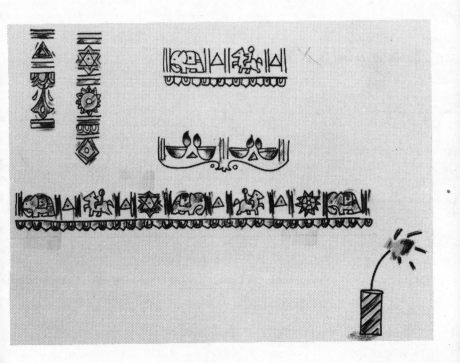

THE HIDDEN GIFT

Subbu sat on the narrow pavement of the bazaar in Ulsoor. It was still early in the morning. The

vendors had not yet begun to call out, but in a little while everything would be moving quickly and he would have to get away from that corner of the street,

before he was trampled upon by the roughshod feet that passed. It was a busy thoroughfare and nobody had time for a little boy who always got in the way.

But, alas, Subbu was different. His left foot was lame. He never could remember how it happened to him, he merely observed that he was different from all the other boys he saw. He could not run behind

the carts that carried mangoes to the bazaar. Nor could he fly the bright kites that he loved to see in the sky. Right now it didn't matter, because he moved away quietly to the steps of the temple and from out of his pocket, he pulled a piece of sugar cane. Oh, how happy he was when he could bite at the sweet juicy stick. He was really happy to sit and chew on it as he watched the passersby.

Today there was a sense of excitement. It was Divali, the festival of lights, and the street was beginning to fill with gaily dressed people. The girls had fresh flowers in their hair and the men were out in their new clothes. People streamed to the temple to worship and had with them small offerings for the gods. Sud-

denly, Subbu felt a gentle hand on his shoulder. A kind old lady bent over him with tears in her eyes. "Here you are," she said. "Here is a rupee to buy yourself some sweets. This day, last year, my grandson died. He was just like you. You are blessed that you have survived. Perhaps the gods have much in store for you." Subbu couldn't believe his eyes. One rupee was a fortune. He had never held one rupee in his hand before. He could not express himself in words, but the old lady saw the gratitude in his eyes and was happy.

Subbu held on to his money. He would only spend a very small portion of it. What he wanted more than anything else was to buy one of those big noisy Divali crackers and set it alight. Yes, yes, he thought, I will buy only one very big cracker and light it myself.

Subbu limped along as fast as he could to the square where there was a quick sale of firecrackers. He was dazzled by the color and the spectacle of hundreds of boxes and packets filled with the most exciting collec-

21

tion of crackers. He asked for the loudest cracker he could buy and came away strangely impressed by the small pellet attached to a wick.

When it was dark at night and the stars were bright, he came out into the noisy street. There was laughter, merriment, and cheer everywhere. People jostled each other on the pavement; vendors were doing good business.

There were lots of nice things to buy, sweets, toys, and fruit; Subbu clutched his cracker. He was looking for a place to set it alight. Ah, he thought, I shall move to that corner. He crouched down and set fire to the cracker. Suddenly there was a tremendous flash

of white light, so bright that night had become day.
Subbu backed away and moved fast and quickly. He

was afraid and so he ran, ran, ran, as fast as he could. He could hardly believe that his legs were taking him so fast. The inert muscles in his leg had suddenly become active. He stopped. His joy knew no words.

He looked around. There was nobody he could speak to. He was so excited, so happy. How he longed to tell somebody that the best thing in the world had happened to him. He had two good feet just like everybody else around him.